D0771316

THE SCARLET FLOWER

THE SCARLET FLOWER

A RUSSIAN FOLK TALE

Told by SERGEI AKSAKOV

Translated from the Russian by ISADORA LEVIN

Illustrations by BORIS DIODOROV

HARCOURT BRACE JOVANOVICH, PUBLISHERS

San Diego New York London

HBJ

Library of Congress Cataloging-in-Publication Data

Aksakov, S. T. (Sergei Timofeevich), 1791–1859.
[Alen'kiĭ tsvetochek. English]
The scarlet flower: a Russian folk tale/told by Sergei Aksakov;
translated from the Russian by Isadora Levin;
illustrations by Boris Diodorov.
p. cm.
Translation of: Alen'kiĭ tsvetochek.
Summary: A young woman's love
transforms a monster into a handsome prince
in this retelling of a classic Russian folktale
version of "Beauty and the Beast."
ISBN 0-15-270487-6
[1. Fairy tales. 2. Folklore — Soviet Union.]
I. Diodorov, Boris, ill. II. Title.
PZ8.A33Sc 1989
398.2'1'0947 — dc19 88-17733
First edition
A B C D E

The Scarlet Flower

ONCE UPON A TIME, in a kingdom far away, there lived a worthy merchant. He had riches of every kind, treasures from over the seas, pearls, precious stones, and gold and silver. He also had three daughters, each one a rare beauty, and the youngest was the fairest of all. The merchant's daughters were dearer to him than all his riches, his pearls, his precious stones, and his gold and silver. But he loved his youngest daughter best, for she gave him the greatest love and was the fairest.

One day, as the worthy merchant was preparing to journey beyond the seas to lands far away, he called his gentle daughters to him and said: "My dear daughters, my sweet and comely daughters, I am departing on a long journey to lands far away. I do not know how long it will take, so I bid you live in peace and honor while I am away. If you do my bidding, I shall bring you whatever gifts you desire. You may have three days to decide, and then you must tell me what your gifts shall be."

The three daughters thought for three days and three nights and then returned to their father.

The eldest daughter bowed to the ground before him and spoke first. "Oh, dear Father, I do not desire brocades of gold and silver, or black sable furs from Siberia, or necklaces of Burmese pearls. Please bring me only a wreath of gold studded with precious stones that shines with a light no less bright than the noonday sun so that the dead of night may become as bright as day." The worthy

merchant thought for a moment and then replied: "Very well, my dear daughter, my sweet and comely daughter. I shall bring you such a wreath from the princess beyond the seas, who has hidden it in a stone treasure house. The treasure house is inside a great rock three meters down, behind three iron doors fastened by three strong locks. The task will be no easy one, but my fortune is great, and I can afford the expense."

Then the middle daughter bowed to the ground before her father and spoke. "Oh, dear Father, I do not desire brocades of gold and silver, or black sable furs from Siberia, or necklaces of Burmese pearls, or a wreath of gold studded with precious stones. Please bring me only a mirror made of a single flawless crystal from the Orient, which will show me all the beauty on earth and in which my own beauty will never age."

The worthy merchant thought for a moment and then replied: "Very well, my dear daughter, my sweet and comely daughter. I shall bring you such a mirror from the King of Persia's daughter, who is so beautiful that no tongue can describe her beauty, no pen depict it, and no man imagine it. She has hidden the mirror in a tall stone tower that stands on a rocky mountain three hundred meters high, behind seven iron doors fastened by seven strong locks, and keeps the keys hanging from her belt. Three thousand steps lead up to the tower, and on each step a Persian soldier stands with sabre drawn, and each sabre is made of finest steel. The task is yet harder than that of your sister, but my fortune is great and I can afford the expense."

Finally the youngest daughter bowed to the ground before her father and spoke. "Oh, dear Father, I do not desire brocades of gold and silver, or black sable furs from Siberia, or necklaces of Burmese pearls, or a wreath of gold studded with precious stones, or a mirror made of a single flawless crystal. Please bring me only a scarlet flower so beautiful that none can equal it in the whole wide world."

The worthy merchant thought longer than before, then kissed his youngest daughter, his favorite, and replied: "You have set me a far harder task than your sisters. It is a simple matter to find a scarlet flower, but how can I ever be sure that none can equal it in the whole wide world? I shall do my best, but you must forgive me if I do not succeed."

He dismissed his sweet and comely daughters and departed on his long journey to lands far away.

THE MERCHANT TRAVELED beyond the seas to strange countries, across kingdoms he had never before seen. He sold his goods for three times their value and paid three times less for the goods he purchased. He traded his wares profitably and collected much gold and silver. When his business was finished, he loaded his ships and sent them home.

Then the merchant obtained the wreath with the precious stones that his eldest daughter desired, and truly it transformed the darkness of night into broad daylight. He obtained the crystal mirror that his middle daughter desired, in which one could see all that was most beautiful on earth and in which a maiden's beauty would not age. But he could not find the gift his youngest and favorite daughter desired — the scarlet flower so beautiful that none could equal it in the whole wide world.

He searched in the gardens of emperors and kings and sultans, and he found many scarlet flowers of surpassing beauty. But who could warrant that there was no other in the whole wide world as beautiful?

He traveled with his faithful servants through dry deserts and dense forests, where they were suddenly set upon by robbers. Thinking it better to let wild beasts tear him

limb from limb than to fall into the hands of robbers, the worthy merchant fled alone deeper into the dark forest.

As the merchant wandered ever deeper, the forest became so dense that it seemed almost impossible for a person to walk through it. Yet the farther he walked, the easier the path became, almost as if the trees were making way for him and the bushes moving apart to let him through. He looked behind him and saw that there was not enough room to thrust a hand through the thicket. He looked to his right and to his left and saw that not even a hare could leap through the tree stumps and fallen branches. The merchant could not understand what was happening, but he walked on and on, down the path that was now smooth and even.

He walked on from morning to night and did not once hear the roar of a wild beast, the hiss of a snake, the hoot of an owl, or the warble of a bird. All was silent. A night as dark as pitch fell, but the path underfoot remained light and clear. He walked on until midnight, when he saw a bright glow ahead, moving toward him. "The forest must be on fire," he thought.

He turned to go back, but his path was blocked by the dense forest. Only straight ahead was the path smooth. "I must stop

here," he thought. "Perhaps the glow will move away or go out altogether."

The merchant stood still and waited, but the glow continued to move toward him. As it came closer, the night around him grew lighter and lighter. The merchant walked on, for he thought, "One cannot die twice, but to die once is inevitable."

The farther he walked, the lighter it grew, until the night was almost as light as noon. Still there was no sound to be heard — not even the crackling of a fire. At last he came to a clearing, and in the middle stood a palace bathed in light, ablaze with silver and gold and precious stones. The palace gleamed with such brilliance that it hurt to look upon it, as if it were on fire, but no fire was to be seen. All the windows were thrown wide open, and sweet music, such as the worthy merchant had never before heard, was playing within.

He entered through the massive open gates and continued up a path of white marble between large and small fountains shooting jets of water high into the air. He entered the palace and climbed stairs covered with thick red carpet and flanked by gilded banisters. He went into the first chamber, but there was no one there. He tried another, and another, and another, until he had entered ten rooms, but there was no one in

them. Everywhere the furnishings were regal, of gold and silver and crystal, such as he had never before seen.

The music continued to play without pause. The merchant said to himself, "This is all very well, but there is nothing to eat." Immediately before him rose a table covered with gold and silver dishes filled with delicate foods and sweetmeats, crystal goblets of wines from over the seas, and honeyed drinks. The merchant seated himself at the table to eat and drink his fill, for he had been wandering across the sands and through the forest for a full day and night, and he was ravenous. He rose from the table, but found no one to thank for the princely feast. No sooner had he risen than the table disappeared, but the music continued to play.

The merchant was greatly amazed by these wonders and continued to walk through the richly furnished chambers. He admired all the treasures but was very tired and thought, "How I wish I could lie down for a bit and maybe even snore a little." Immediately before him stood a canopied bed of pure chased gold, with legs of crystal and bed curtains of silver cloth fringed with tassels of pearls. On the bed, like a small hill, lay a featherbed of the softest swansdown.

The merchant lay down on the featherbed of swansdown and drew the silver curtains, which felt as fine and soft as silk. The chamber grew dark, as though it were twilight, and the music now sounded from afar. The merchant thought, "Ah, if only I could see my daughters, even in a dream!" And then he fell asleep.

WHEN HE AWOKE, the sun was already above the trees. All through the night he had dreamed of his sweet and gentle daughters. His two older daughters were merry as can be, but his youngest, his favorite, daughter was sorrowful. The older daughters had suitors and intended to marry without awaiting their father's blessing. His youngest, his favorite, daughter, the rarest of rare beauties, would hear no suitor until her own dear father returned. At heart, the merchant was both happy and unhappy.

A suit of clothes was laid out for him near a fountain playing in a pool of crystal. He dressed and washed but was no longer amazed by the newest wonders. On a table tea and coffee were laid out, and the daintiest sweetmeats. He ate, then walked again through the chambers to admire them once more by the light of day. The wondrous palace seemed even finer to him than it had the night before. Through the open windows he saw luxuriant gardens filled with exotic plants and flowers of indescribable beauty. He was seized with a desire to walk through the gardens and examine them more closely.

He went down a staircase of green marble and copper malachite straight into the verdant gardens. Fruit, ripe and red, hung from the trees, making his mouth water. Lovely flowers with double petals and rare fragrances blossomed, and over them hovered many-colored birds with feathers that looked like green and crimson velvet sprinkled with gold and silver. The birds sang divine songs; the fountains played so high that you could not see their tops; and clear springs rippled and bubbled along beds of crystal.

The worthy merchant looked at all these marvels and did not know on which to rest his gaze. He heard the divine songs and did not know which bird to listen to. In a daze he strolled through the garden. Suddenly he saw a flower blooming on a grassy knoll — a scarlet flower of unbelievable beauty, so exquisite that no tongue could describe it nor pen depict it. The merchant's heart missed a beat. As he neared the flower, its fragrance flowed over him like a stream. The merchant trembled from head to foot and exclaimed in joy: "Here is the scarlet flower so beautiful that none can equal it in the whole wide world. This is the flower that

my youngest, my favorite, daughter desired that I bring her."

With these words, he plucked the flower. That same instant, lightning flashed from the clear blue sky and thunder shook the earth. As if out of the ground there rose before him a monster, neither man nor beast, but hairy and horrible to behold.

The monster roared in a savage voice: "What have you done? How dare you pluck from my garden the precious flower that I love? I have guarded it jealously, for my only comfort is to gaze upon it. Now you have deprived me of the one delight of my life. It is I who am master of this palace and its gardens. It is I who have received you as a dear and welcome guest, I who have given you food and drink and a bed to sleep on. Is this how you repay me for my hospitality? Hear your bitter fate! You shall die an untimely death for the wrong you have done me!"

And from all around, thousands of savage voices echoed, "You shall die an untimely death!"

The worthy merchant trembled with fear. He looked around and saw countless evil creatures creeping toward him from under every bush, out of the water, and up from the earth. He fell upon his knees before the monster and beseeched him piteously.

"Oh, gracious lord, monster of the forest and the sea!" he said. "Please have pity on me. Forgive me for unwittingly committing this offense against you and allow me to say a word in my own defense. I have three daughters, three beautiful daughters, sweet and gentle, and to each I promised a gift: a bejeweled wreath for my eldest daughter, a crystal mirror for my middle daughter, and for my youngest daughter a scarlet flower so beautiful that none can equal it in the whole wide world. I did not think that such a great lord, so wealthy a nobleman, would begrudge me the scarlet flower that my youngest and favorite daughter desired. Pardon me, foolish man that I am. Let me return to my dear daughters and take with me the scarlet flower for my youngest and favorite daughter, and I shall repay you with as much gold as you shall require."

A roar of laughter like a thunderclap resounded through the forest, and the monster of the forest and the sea said to the merchant: "I have no need for your gold. You shall have no mercy from me, and I shall have my loyal servants tear you to pieces, to small pieces. But there is one way to save yourself. I shall let you go home, free and unharmed, reward you with countless riches, and give you the scarlet flower if you will send me one of your sweet and gentle daughters. I shall do her no harm, and she shall live in honor and freedom in my palace. I am weary of living alone and wish to have a companion."

The worthy merchant threw himself upon the cold ground and wept bitter tears. He looked at the monster of the forest and the sea, and he thought of his daughters, his sweet and gentle daughters, and uttered even more piteous cries. For a long time he beat his breast and wept, and then he said in a woeful voice: "Gracious lord, monster of the forest and the sea! What if one of my sweet, gentle daughters will not come to you of her own free will? Do you expect me to bind her hand and foot and send her by force? And how will she find her way here? It has taken me two years to arrive at your palace, and by what route I do not know."

The monster of the forest and the sea replied: "I do not want a prisoner! Your daughter must come of her own free will, out of her love for you. If one of your daughters will not come, then you must return yourself to die a cruel death. Take this ring from my finger. Whoever wears it on the little finger of his right hand will find himself wherever he wishes to be. I give you three days and three nights before you or one of your daughters must return to me."

The merchant replied: "It is best that I see my daughters and give them my blessing. If they do not wish to save me from death, I

will have time to prepare for it before returning to you." As the merchant spoke these words, the monster of the forest and the sea took the gold ring from his finger and handed it to him.

THE WORTHY MERCHANT put the ring on the little finger of his right hand and immediately found himself at the entrance to his own courtyard. The same moment, his faithful servants drove his richly laden caravans through the gates. The house was filled with noise and bustle, and the three daughters greeted their father with great joy.

They noticed that their father was not gladdened by their attentions and seemed to be hiding a secret grief. The older sisters asked if he had perhaps lost his great riches, but the youngest gave no thought to the riches and said: "Riches may come and go and may be acquired anew. Tell me, please, what canker is eating at your heart!"

Then the worthy merchant said to his daughters, his sweet and gentle daughters: "Do not fear. I have not lost my great riches but have increased them threefold or more. I have quite another sorrow, but that can wait until tomorrow. Today, let us make merry!"

He bade his servants bring forth the iron-bound chests from the caravan, and he gave

to his eldest daughter the wreath of gold studded with precious stones. He gave to his middle daughter the mirror of crystal, and to his youngest daughter he gave a golden bowl with the scarlet flower. The older daughters were elated and took their gifts away to their chambers, but the youngest daughter trembled all over at the sight of the scarlet flower and wept as if with foreboding. Her father said: "Oh, my youngest daughter, my favorite daughter, why do you not take the flower that you so desired? There is none that can equal it in the whole wide world."

The youngest daughter took the scarlet flower unwillingly and kissed her father's hands, weeping bitterly. Soon the older daughters returned, and they all sat down at the oaken tables covered with embroidered cloths and laden with delicacies and honeyed drinks. They ate and drank and conversed together lovingly.

That evening the merchant's house was filled with kinsmen and welcome guests and others seeking the merchant's favors. Their lavish dinner was served on dishes of gold and silver. Never before had the guests beheld such magnificence. Their talk and feasting continued late into the night.

The following morning the worthy merchant sent for his eldest daughter and told her of all that had befallen him. He asked if she would save him from a cruel death by going to live in the palace of the monster of the forest and the sea.

His eldest daughter refused, saying, "The daughter who should save you is the one for whom you plucked the scarlet flower."

The worthy merchant then sent for his middle daughter and told her of all that had befallen him. He asked if she would save him from a cruel death by going to live in the palace of the monster of the forest and the sea.

His middle daughter refused, saying, "The daughter who should save you is the one for whom you plucked the scarlet flower."

Then the worthy merchant sent for his youngest daughter and began to tell her of all that had befallen him, but before he could finish his tale, his youngest, his favorite, daughter fell upon her knees before him and said: "Give me your blessing, oh, dear Father. I will go to the monster of the forest and the sea and live in his palace. It was for me that you plucked the scarlet flower, and it is I who must save you."

The worthy merchant wept and embraced his youngest, his favorite, daughter and said: "My sweet one, my gentlest and

most beloved of daughters, you have my blessing for saving me from a cruel death by going of your own free will to live in the palace of the monster of the forest and the sea. You will live in great luxury and freedom, but no one knows where the palace is, and it is surrounded by a forest so dense that there is no way to reach it on horseback or on foot — not even the swift-leaping hare or the bird on the wing can find its way through. We will have no news from you, nor will we be able to send you news of us. How will I live out my bitter days without seeing your sweet face or hearing your tender voice? Alas, I am parting from you forever."

His youngest, his favorite, daughter then replied: "Oh, dear Father, do not weep, do not grieve, for I will be living in luxury and freedom. I will not fear the monster of the forest and the sea but will serve him faithfully. I will carry out his will, and perhaps he will have mercy on me. Do not mourn me as if I were dead, for it may be that one day I will return to you."

The worthy merchant wept and sobbed, finding no comfort in his daughter's words.

Then her sisters filled the house with the sound of their weeping, as if to say, "See how unhappy we are, how sorry for our dear younger sister." But the youngest daughter neither wept nor sighed but made preparations for her journey into the unknown.

The third day and the third night passed, and the time came for the worthy merchant to part with his youngest, his favorite, daughter. He kissed her and wept bitter tears as he gave her his blessing. Then he took the ring that the monster of the forest and the sea had given him and put it on the little finger of his youngest, his favorite, daughter's right hand. She instantly vanished with all her possessions.

SHE FOUND HERSELF in the palace of the monster of the forest and the sea, on a bedstead of chased gold with crystal legs, lying on a featherbed of swansdown with a coverlet embroidered with thread of gold and silver. Sweet music was playing, such as she had never before heard.

She rose from the swansdown bed and saw all her belongings and the scarlet flower in the golden bowl set out on tables of copper malachite. The chamber was filled with beautiful and useful things: chairs upon which to sit, couches upon which to recline, fine clothing to wear. One wall was all mirror, another was made of gold, a third of silver, and a fourth of ivory and mammoth tusks set with rubies and sapphires. As she looked around, she thought, "This must be my bedchamber."

She was seized by a desire to see all of the palace and went to inspect its spacious halls and chambers. As she walked, she marveled at its treasures; each chamber was more beautiful than the last, exceeding in beauty even the description her dear father had given her. She took the scarlet flower from its golden bowl and walked out into the verdant gardens. The birds sang their divine melodies to her, and the trees and bushes nodded as if they were greeting her, the fountains played ever higher, and the springs rippled in their beds of crystal. She walked to the grassy knoll from which the worthy merchant had plucked the scarlet flower that had none to equal it in the whole wide world. She put out her hand to place the flower into the earth once again, but the flower flew out of her hand to join itself to its stalk and began blossoming even more beautifully than before.

She marveled anew and was glad for the scarlet flower that she had so greatly desired. She returned to the palace and found a table set with a sumptuous meal. She thought, "Perhaps the monster of the forest and the sea is not angry with me and will be a merciful master." No sooner had she thought this than a message appeared in letters of fire across the white marble wall:

I am no master of yours, but your obedient slave. It is you who are my mistress, to command me. All

that you desire, any whim that may enter your head, I am here to fulfill.

She read the fiery words, which then vanished from the wall as if they had never been. It entered her head that she should write to her father so that he might have news of her. No sooner had the thought come to her than paper, a golden pen, and an inkpot appeared before her. And so she wrote to her father and her sweet and gentle sisters:

Do not weep or grieve for me. I live like a princess in the palace of the monster of the forest and the sea, who writes fiery messages on a white marble wall but whom I never see or hear. He knows all that passes through my mind and fulfills all my wishes instantly. He does not wish me to call him master, but calls me his mistress.

No sooner had she written the letter and sealed it than it disappeared from her hands, as if it had never been there. The music played more sweetly than before, and she sat down to her meal in the best of spirits. She ate and drank, enjoying the delicate foods and the sweet music. After her meal, she went to her chamber to lie down, and the music played softly, that it might not disturb her as she slept.

She awoke in a merry mood and walked again in the verdant gardens to examine their wonders more closely. The trees and flowers nodded to her, and the ripe pears and peaches and apples flew to her mouth. At

eventide she returned to her chamber, where the table was again laid with delicate foods and honeyed drinks.

After her supper, she returned to the chamber with the white marble wall and found another message in words of fire.

Is my mistress content with her gardens, her apartments, her fare, and her servant?

And the merchant's young daughter, the rare beauty, said wistfully: "Do not call me your mistress, but ever be my kind master, gentle and merciful. I will never transgress your will, for I am grateful to you for all you give me. There are no apartments or verdant gardens in the whole wide world to equal yours, so how could I fail but be content? Never have I seen such marvels, and I am overcome with amazement. But, dear master, I am afraid to sleep in solitude, and in all your palace there is not a soul to talk to."

Then these words appeared in fire upon the wall:

Have no fear, my fair mistress. You will not sleep in solitude, for your own faithful maid now awaits you. There are many servants in these apartments, but you cannot see or hear them. With me, they will guard you night and day. We will not allow the wind to ruffle a hair on your head or a speck of dust to settle on you.

When the merchant's sweet and gentle daughter returned to her bedchamber, whom did she see there but her faithful maid, shaking and ill with fear. At the sight of her mistress, the maid rejoiced greatly and kissed her white hands and embraced her little feet. Her mistress was just as delighted to see her and asked after her dear father and her sisters. Then she recounted all that had befallen her during this time. Talking and embracing, they did not fall asleep until the first streaks of dawn.

IN THIS WAY the time passed. Each day rich new dresses awaited the merchant's daughter, and priceless new ornaments such as no tongue could describe nor pen depict. Each day the food and entertainment were new and magnificent. She rode through the dense, dark forest in a chariot with neither horses nor harness to the strains of sweet music, and the trees parted before her to a broad, smooth road. She embroidered silk with silver and gold thread and decorated it with fringes of pearls. She sent presents to her dear father and made a present of the most richly embroidered silk to her gentle master, the monster of the forest and the sea. And with every passing day, she went more and more often to the white marble chamber to speak affectionately with him and to read his messages in fiery writing on the wall.

The merchant's young daughter, the rare beauty, grew accustomed to this way of liv-

ing and no longer marveled or wondered or feared. The invisible servants attended to her every wish, handing her whatever she needed, driving her in the chariot without horses, playing music for her, and carrying out her every order. And her gentle master grew dearer to her each day. She saw that it was not without reason that he called her his dear mistress and that he loved her more than he loved himself. She desired to hear his voice and speak with him without going to the white marble chamber to read the fiery words.

She would ask, even beg, him to accord her this favor, but the monster of the forest and the sea would not grant her request, for he feared his voice would frighten her. Finally, he could withstand her pleas no longer, and for the last time wrote in fiery letters on the white marble wall:

Go to the verdant gardens today, seat yourself in your favorite arbor with its twining leaves and twigs and blossoms, and say, "Speak to me, my faithful slave."

And the merchant's young daughter, the rare beauty, ran out to the verdant gardens, entered her favorite arbor with its twining leaves and twigs and blossoms, seated herself on the brocade-covered bench, and said breathlessly, her heart beating like that of a trapped bird: "Do not fear, my master, my kind, gentle master, that you will frighten me with your voice. After all your kindness I would not be afraid of the roar of a wild beast. Speak to me without fear!"

She heard a sigh behind the arbor, then a terrifying voice, a savage bellow, hoarse and husky — even though the monster of the forest and the sea was speaking in a lowered voice. At the sound, the merchant's daughter, the rare beauty, gave a start, then overcame her fear and gave no further sign of it. Soon she was listening only to his gentle, tender speeches, his clever, wise words, and her heart filled with delight.

From that time on they conversed whole days on end as she walked through the verdant gardens and in the chambers of the palace, or drove through the dense, dark forest. No sooner would she say, "Are you there, my kind, dear master?" than the monster of the forest and the sea would answer, "Your faithful slave, your constant friend, is here, my lovely lady."

AND SO THE TIME passed pleasantly, and then the merchant's young daughter, the rare beauty, desired to look upon the monster of the forest and the sea with her own eyes. She begged and pleaded with him to allow her to see him, but he would not agree, for he feared his appearance would frighten her. He was such a fearsome sight that even wild beasts fled to their dens to hide. So the monster of the forest and the sea said to her: "Do not ask of me, my fair mistress, my beloved, beautiful mistress, that I show you my loathsome countenance and my hideous body. You have grown accustomed to my voice, and we are friends. We are hardly ever apart, and you love me for the infinite love I bear you, but should you see me in all my repulsive hideousness, you will hate the unfortunate being that I am and will drive me from your sight. And if I cannot be near you, I will die of grief."

The merchant's young daughter would not listen and pleaded even more urgently. She swore that the most hideous monster in the world would not frighten her, for she would never lose affection for her gentle master.

"If you are an old man," she said, "you will be my grandfather. If you are middle-aged, you will be my uncle. And if you are young, you will be my brother, and as long as I live, you will be my dear friend."

The monster of the forest and the sea did not yield for a long time, but in the end he

could not withstand her supplications and her tears, and he said, "I cannot deny you, for I love you more than I love myself. I will give you your desire, although I know it will destroy my happiness and I will die. Come to the verdant gardens in the dim twilight when the red sun has set behind the forest, and say, 'Appear to me, faithful friend,' and I will show you my repulsive, loathsome countenance and my hideous body. If you should not find the strength to remain with me any longer, I will not keep you in eternal bondage and torment. You will find, under your pillow, my gold ring. Place it on the little finger of your right hand, and you will find yourself in your dear father's home and will never hear of me again."

The merchant's young daughter, the rare beauty, felt no fear. Without a moment's hesitation, she went to the verdant garden to await the appointed hour. When twilight fell and the red sun set behind the forest, she pronounced these words, "Appear to me, faithful friend!" From afar appeared the monster of the forest and the sea; he crossed the road and disappeared into the thicket. The merchant's young daughter felt such a shock that she threw up her white hands and let out a heartrending cry as she fell fainting to the ground. The monster of the forest and the sea was indeed fearsome to see. His arms were crooked, his hands were the claws of a wild beast, his legs were those of a horse, he had two large humps like those of a camel in front and behind, and he was covered with hair from head to foot. A boar's fangs protruded from his mouth, his nose was hooked like the beak of the golden eagle, and his eyes were those of an owl.

When she came to herself, the merchant's young daughter heard someone beside her weeping bitterly and saying piteously: "You have undone me, my beloved mistress. I will never again behold your fair face, for you will not even wish to hear my voice. I will die of grief."

She felt sorry and ashamed, and she overcame her terrible fear. Controlling the beating of her heart, she said: "No, do not fear, my kind and gentle master. I will never again be afraid of your fearsome appearance and will not part from you or forget your kindness. Appear to me once more as you are; it was only at first that I was afraid."

The monster of the forest and the sea appeared to her once more, but he would not come near until she called him to her. They walked about until late at night and conversed tenderly. And the merchant's daughter, the rare beauty, felt no fear. The next morning she saw the monster of the forest and the sea in the full light of day,

and although she was frightened at first, she gave no sign of it, and soon her fear disappeared. Now they conversed even more than before, hardly parting for days at a time, dining together on delicate morsels, and refreshing themselves with honeyed drinks. They walked through the verdant gardens and drove in the chariot without horses through the dense, dark forest.

AND SO THE TIME passed pleasantly. One night the merchant's young daughter, the rare beauty, dreamed that her father was lying ill, and a terrible grief seized her. When the monster of the forest and the sea saw her sad and tearful, he was distressed and asked her why she wept. She told him of her sad dream and asked his permission to go to her dear father and gentle sisters. The monster of the forest and the sea replied, "Why do you ask my permission? My gold ring lies under your pillow. Place it on the little finger of your right hand, and you will find yourself in your dear father's house. Stay with him as long as you are happy there. I will say only this: if you do not return in exactly three days and three nights, I will no longer be alive. I will die the same minute, for I love you more than I love myself, and I cannot live without you."

She assured him with tender words and vows that she would return exactly one hour before the three days and three nights had passed. She bade her kind, gentle master farewell, slipped the gold ring on the little finger of her right hand, and found herself in the large courtyard of her father, the worthy merchant. As she stepped onto the high porch of his fine house, all the servants rushed to her with cries and exclamations. Her sweet and gentle sisters ran to her, too, and were amazed by her maidenly beauty and royal attire. They took her white hands and led her to her dear father's bed, where he lay, ill and unhappy, thinking of her and weeping bitter tears. When he beheld his youngest, his favorite, daughter, he was beside himself with joy, and he, too, was amazed by her maidenly beauty and royal attire.

For a long time they kissed and spoke tenderly to one another. The merchant's young daughter, the rare beauty, told her dear father and her sisters how she lived in the palace of the monster of the forest and the sea. She told them all from beginning to end, concealing nothing. And the worthy merchant rejoiced greatly to hear of her rich and regal life. He wondered that she was able to look at her hideous master without fear, for he himself shook and trembled when he recalled the sight of the monster of the forest and the sea. But when her sisters heard of her untold wealth and her queenly power, they grew envious.

The first day passed like an hour, the second like a minute, and on the third day, the older sisters tried to persuade their younger sister not to return to the monster of the forest and the sea. "Let him perish," they said. "It will be good riddance."

But their younger sister grew angry and replied, "If I should repay my kind, gentle lord for all his kindness and great, nay, his boundless, love by causing him to die of grief, I would not want to go on living. I would deserve to be thrown to the wild beasts and torn apart."

Her father, the worthy merchant, praised her for speaking so well, and they decided she would, indeed, return to the monster of the forest and the sea exactly one hour before the appointed time. But the older sisters were vexed and thought of an evil trick. They set all the clocks in the house back one hour. And the worthy merchant and all the servants knew nothing of what they had done.

At the appointed hour, the merchant's young daughter, the rare beauty, felt a great

pain in her heart, as if a hand were pulling her away. She looked at her father's clocks, first at the English ones, then the German ones, but found it was still too early to start on her journey. Her sisters chattered to her and asked questions in order to delay her. But her heart could not stand it, and the merchant's youngest daughter, the rare beauty, bade farewell to her dear father, the worthy merchant, and received his blessing. She bade farewell to her sisters and to the faithful servants. Then without waiting another minute for the hour to strike, she placed the gold ring on the little finger of her right hand and found herself in the great palace of the monster of the forest and the sea. Surprised that he had not hastened to greet her, she cried, "Where are you my kind lord, my true friend? Why have you not come to meet me? I have returned one whole hour and one minute before the appointed time."

No answer came. The silence was complete: the birds were not singing their divine songs in the verdant gardens, the fountains were not playing, the spring was not rippling, and there was no music in the palace chambers. Her heart missed a beat. She sensed great evil. She ran through all the spacious halls and chambers, through the

verdant gardens, calling her gentle master, but no answer came, no obedient voice replied. She ran to the grassy knoll where her beloved scarlet flower bloomed in all its splendor. There she beheld the monster of the forest and the sea lying with the scarlet flower clasped in his hideous paws. He seemed to have fallen into a slumber while he awaited her, and the merchant's young daughter, the rare beauty, tried to awaken him gently, but he did not hear her. She tried again to awaken him and seized his hairy paw. Then she saw that the monster of the forest and the sea breathed no more; he lay there as one dead.

Her clear eyes dimmed, her legs gave way under her, and she fell to her knees and embraced her gentle lord's head in her white arms, his hideous, repulsive head, and sobbed, "Arise, awake my dearest friend. I love you as I would my betrothed!"

No sooner had she uttered these words than lightning flashed, the earth quaked with a mighty roll of thunder, and a bolt struck the grassy knoll. The merchant's youngest daughter, the rare beauty, fell fainting to the ground. When she awoke, she was sitting in the white marble chamber on a throne of gold and precious stones. Holding her in his arms was a young prince, the handsomest

one could imagine, attired in cloth of gold with an emperor's crown upon his head. Before him stood her father and her sisters, and all round knelt courtiers dressed in gold and silver brocade. The young prince, the handsome young prince, said to her: "You came to care for me, my fair beloved, when I was a hideous monster because I was gentle and loved you. Try to love me now in my human form. Be the bride I have longed for. When he was alive, my father, who was a mighty king of great renown, angered an evil sorceress, who stole me away when I was yet an infant. With her devilish powers the sorceress transformed me into that frightful beast and laid a curse upon me that I must live as a monster, hideous and repulsive to all God's creatures, until a fair maiden came who would love me in that fearsome state and desire to become my wife. Then the evil curse would be lifted, and I would become once more a prince of pleasing countenance. I have lived as a fearsome monster, terrifying all for many years, wishing only for a fair maiden who would love me. But you alone loved me, hideous and repulsive monster that I was, for my gentleness and kindness and my undying love for you. For that you shall be the wife of a king of great renown and queen of a mighty land."

All were amazed at this strange story, and the courtiers bowed low, to the very ground. The worthy merchant bestowed his blessing upon his youngest, his favorite, daughter, the rare beauty, and upon the crown prince. The envious older sisters congratulated the bride and groom, as did all the great lords and noble knights. Without more ado they celebrated the wedding and sat down to a merry feast. The handsome prince and the merchant's youngest daughter, the rare beauty, lived happily ever after.

The illustrations in this book were done in watercolor on Arches paper.

The display type is set in Castellar.

The text type is set in Centaur.

Composition by Thompson Type, San Diego, California

Color separations were made by Bright Arts, Ltd., Hong Kong.

Printed and bound by Tien Wah Press, Singapore

Production supervision by Warren Wallerstein and Eileen McGlone

Designed by Michael Farmer